Hidden Pumpkins

Written by Anne Margaret Lewis

Illustrated by Jim DeWildt

Mackinac Island Press

for the love of reading

For my four children, Caitlin, Matthew, Patrick, and Cameron who inspired this very Halloween book. Halloween is always a favorite time for our family, from carving pumpkins to dressing up to trick-or-treating. Thank you, kids, for always making Halloween fun.

Anne Margaret Lewis

For my sister, Marcella, who always has a hug and a smile for everyone.

Jim DeWildt

Text Copyright © 2005 by Anne Margaret Lewis
Illustration Copyright © by Jim DeWildt

First Edition

Library of Congress Cataloging-in-Publication Data

Lewis, Anne Margaret and DeWildt, Jim
Hidden Pumpkins

Summary: A Halloween seek and find children's book with 100 hidden Mr. Pumpkins and many more hidden Halloween treasures.
ISBN 0-9749145-5-X
Fiction

10 9 8 7 6 5 4 3 2 1

Printed and bound in Canada by Friesens, Altona, Manitoba.

A Mackinac Island Press, Inc. publication
www.mackinacislandpress.com

I'm Mr. Pumpkin from the great pumpkin patch
There are 100 of me hidden for you to catch

Pumpkins, broomsticks, goblins and witches
Witch's brew, gooey goo and pumpkin pie so delicious

Ghosts, graveyards and skeletons screaming
Headless horsemen, caramel apples, am I just dreaming?

Hayrides, Halloween games
and the great pumpkin patch.
Welcome to Hidden Halloween with
100 Mr. Pumpkins to catch.

Now slo o o w w ly turn the page,
don't be toooo scared…
Start searching for Mr. Pumpkin–
he's hidden everywhere.

Haunted houses with spooky spiders
    and great big spider webs;
    creaking floors, with scurrying mice
    and an old iron creaky bed.

I'm Mr. Pumpkin from the great pumpkin patch,
    there are 8 of me hidden for you to catch.

Trick-or-treat, trick-or-treat,
  give me something good to eat.
Will it be sour? Will it be sweet?
Or will it be icky old smelly feet?

I'm Mr. Pumpkin from the
  great pumpkin patch,
there are 9 of me hidden
  for you to catch.

Orange leaves, red leaves and
  yellow leaves, too;
  piles and piles of leaves at
  Halloween…let's jump…Yahoo!

I'm Mr. Pumpkin from the
  great pumpkin patch,
  there are 9 of me hidden for
  you to catch.

Bobbing for apples at the Halloween bash,
with donuts and cider and the monster mash.

I'm Mr. Pumpkin from the great pumpkin patch,
there are 8 of me hidden for you to catch.

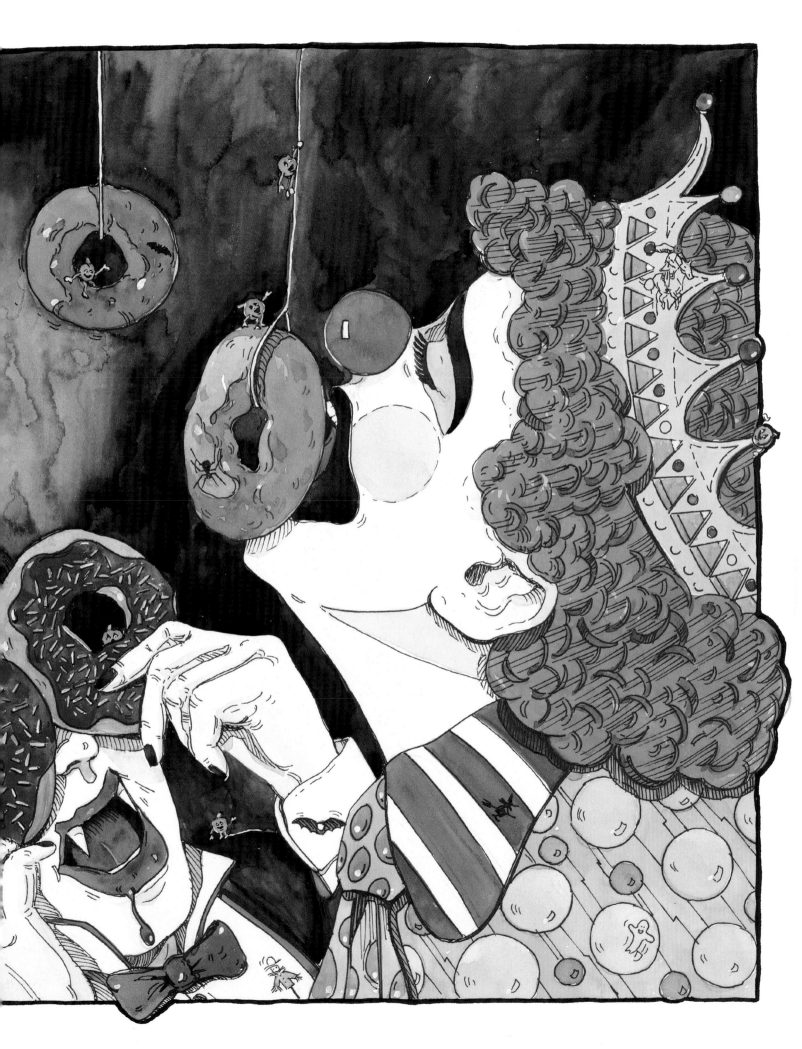

Scary pumpkins, goofy pumpkins and pumpkins looking sad;
pumpkin carving is gooey and fun, I think I'll name mine Jack.

I'm Mr. Pumpkin from the
great pumpkin patch,
there are 6 of me hidden
for you to catch.

Black cats, black bats and a big, old, fat black rat;
a scary old woman, in an old barn, wearing a scary
old witch's hat.

I'm Mr. Pumpkin from the great pumpkin patch,
there are 10 of me hidden for you to catch.

Candy corn and suckers and
great big candy bars.
Which candy shall you choose,
from the Halloween candy jar?

I'm Mr. Pumpkin from the
great pumpkin patch,
there are 7 of me hidden
for you to catch.

Friendly ghosts and ghostly ghosts
    and ghosts with great big grimaces;
    booooing ghosts, howwwling ghosts
    and ghosts blowing…Halloween kisses?

I'm Mr. Pumpkin from the great pumpkin patch,
    there are 8 of me hidden for you to catch.

Haunted trees in the haunted
forest with horrible haunted faces.
They grab at your hair, walk
through if you dare, they'll jump
out from haunted places.

I'm Mr. Pumpkin from the
great pumpkin patch,
there are 7 of me hidden
for you to catch.

Pumpkin pie, pumpkin soup and pumpkin seeds all roasted;
pumpkin spread is delicious, on pumpkin bread all toasted.

I'm Mr. Pumpkin from the great pumpkin patch,
there are 7 of me hidden for you to catch.

Princesses and wizards and goblins
marching in the Halloween parade;
skeletons, vampires and Dorothy too...
so proud on Halloween day.

I'm Mr. Pumpkin from the great pumpkin patch,
there are 6 of me hidden for you to catch.

Werewolves howling with the full moon glowing,
owls whispering a spooky hoot hoo!
The bats are screeching, the mice are scampering...
are you scared of Halloween yet? Boo!

I'm Mr. Pumpkin from the great pumpkin patch,
there are 7 of me hidden for you to catch.

Tiny pumpkins, giant pumpkins, pumpkins on every vine;
too many pumpkins everywhere...which one shall be mine?

I'm Mr. Pumpkin from the great pumpkin patch,
there are 8 of me hidden for you to catch.

Now you've found 100 Mr. Pumpkins in this very Halloween book;
go back to each page and search for more Halloween treasures…
come on, let's take a look.

WITCH ON BROOM

OWL

SCARECROW

CROW

GHOST

HEADLESS HORSEMAN

BAT

CARVED PUMPKIN

SKELETON

BLACK CAT

TRICK OR TREAT BAG

SPIDER

I'm Mr. Cherry, I'm red and plump and round;
there's one of me hidden in *Hidden Pumpkins*
somewhere to be found.

Mr. Cherry is from *Hidden Cherries*, another hidden book,
with lots of cherry treasures to find and lots of fun to look.